No English

by Jacqueline Jules
illustrations by Amy Huntington

Jacqueline Jules

 mitten press

All inquiries should be addressed to:
Mitten Press
An imprint of Ann Arbor Media Group LLC
2500 S. State Street
Ann Arbor, MI 48104

Printed and bound in Canada.

10   9   8   7   6   5   4   3   2

Library of Congress Cataloging-in-Publication Data
Jules, Jacqueline, 1956-
No English / by Jacqueline Jules ;
illustrations by Amy Huntington.
p. cm.
Summary: When Diane behaves unkindly to the new girl from Argentina, not knowing she can
not speak English, she decides to find a way they can communicate and become friends.
ISBN-13: 978-1-58726-474-0 (hardcover)
ISBN-10: 1-58726-474-9
[1. Schools--Fiction. 2. English language--Fiction. 3. Drawing--Fiction.
4. Friendship--Fiction.] I. Huntington, Amy, ill. II. Title.
PZ7.J92947No 2007
[E]--dc22
2006035727

To the students and
staff at Timber Lane
Elementary School
—J.J.

To everyone at
Robinson School
—A.H.

"No English," the new girl said, shaking her head. "Español."

Her name was Blanca and she was from Argentina. Mrs. Bertram gave her the empty desk next to mine.

As soon as she sat down, Blanca took colored pencils out of her backpack. She drew all during spelling and Mrs. Bertram didn't say a word to her. When I got caught making a picture during class, I got in trouble. It didn't seem fair.

"Mrs. Bertram!" I raised my hand. "Blanca is coloring. She's not doing the spelling words."

Blanca looked up to see everyone staring at her. Then the classroom door opened. A lady walked in.

"I'm Mrs. Sanderson," she said. "I'll be helping Blanca learn English."

Everyone watched Blanca walk to the front of the room. She looked scared, like a little kid lost in a shopping mall. I suddenly felt bad for telling on her.

When Blanca left the room,
Mrs. Bertram talked to the class. "Can you
imagine what it's like to be surrounded by people you
don't understand?"

"Lonely," Jessica said.

"Absolutely," Mrs. Bertram said. "What can we do to make
Blanca feel welcome?"

"We could say, 'hola,'" John said. "That's hello in Spanish."

"Good idea," Mrs. Bertram agreed. "What else?"

"I know!" Alison raised her hand. "We could learn about Argentina."

"On the Internet," Bobby added.

Mrs. Bertram let Bobby and Alison use the computer before lunch. They found out that January is summertime in Argentina.

"Weird!" Billy said.

"Just different," Mrs. Bertram corrected.

The more we talked about Blanca and her country, the more I wanted to make up for being a tattletale.

At recess, I saw Blanca on the edge of the blacktop, jumping
rope. Second graders weren't allowed past the third fence post.
I ran across the blacktop to warn her.

When I got there, Blanca was jumping to a Spanish rhyme.
"Uno, dos, tres . . ."

"Hola!" I said, remembering the Spanish word for hello.

Blanca stopped jumping. "Hola!"

This was my chance to make friends. I pointed to the rope.
"Share?"

She smiled and handed the rope to me. Just as I was taking
it, Mrs. Greevy, the playground teacher, called.

"Girls! Come back here!"

I didn't want us to get in trouble. "Come on!" I yelled to Blanca as I ran back.

But Blanca didn't understand. With a cry, she ran up beside me and grabbed the jump rope out of my hands.

"No!" she screamed.

Blanca thought I was trying to steal her rope! I watched her run across the playground and into the school. She was out of trouble with Mrs. Greevy, but it was the second time in one day that I had hurt Blanca's feelings.

It bothered me like a scratchy tag at the back of my neck. How could I make friends with Blanca? She didn't understand when I talked to her.

Blanca sat alone at lunch. On the playground, she kept to herself. Sometimes I watched her jump rope. But I didn't go near her.

Friday afternoon was library time. I got an idea during checkout.

"Mrs. Porter," I asked the librarian. "Do we have any Spanish books?"

"Yes," she said, handing me a book with nice pictures. "This one is in Spanish and English."

I found Blanca sitting at a library table all alone.

"For you," I said, holding out the book.

Blanca shook her head, as if she was saying "no." I opened up the book and pointed at the Spanish words.

"Español!" Her brown eyes lit up.

A second later, I was sitting beside her, putting my finger under a Spanish word. She read it to me. Then she put her finger under an English word and I read aloud. When we left the library, Blanca was carrying the book against her chest, smiling.

On Monday morning, Blanca handed me a picture. It showed two girls sitting at a table reading a book. One of the girls had black hair and brown eyes and looked like Blanca. The other girl had blonde hair and blue eyes like mine.

"Thank you." We smiled at each other.

I picked up my pencil and wrote "Blanca" beside her face and "Diane" beside mine. Blanca had never said my name. I wanted to make sure she knew it.

When I showed the picture to Blanca, we both giggled.

"Please stop talking!"

Mrs. Bertram was not there. We had a substitute named Mrs. Clemons.

"This is spelling time." Mrs. Clemons frowned.

Blanca picked up her colored pencils and started a picture of her family. I made a picture of my family. We labeled everyone. I found out that she had a younger brother named Manuel. She found out that I had a younger sister named Veronica. Then Blanca drew a picture of her house. I made a picture of my house. We leaned toward each other, whispering and pointing.

"Girls!" Mrs. Clemons called out. "This is the second time I've asked you to be quiet."

I couldn't help it. Blanca and I were having such a good time. One small giggle came out—then a louder one. Blanca started giggling, too. Soon, the whole class was laughing with us.

"That's enough!" Mrs. Clemons pointed at Blanca and me. "Come up here right now!"

Everyone stopped giggling. I took Blanca's hand and gently led her to Mrs. Clemons.

"Tell me your names!" she snapped as she filled out a purple card, the card that said you were in trouble and had to visit the office.

"Diane Wells," I squeaked. "And this is Blanca."

"Blanca what?" Mrs. Clemons asked.

"No English," Blanca said, shaking her head.

Mrs. Clemons handed me the purple card. Blanca and I left the classroom for the long walk down the hall.

When we arrived, the secretary asked us to sit down. I put my hands in my lap and tried not to cry. I had never been to the office before.

Mr. Conwell, the assistant principal, walked in. He was so tall, I could hardly see his face from where I was sitting. Blanca put her hand on mine.

"Young ladies," he said in a deep voice. "Come this way."

We sat down in his office with our heads lowered.

"So! What brings you here this morning?"

I lifted my head a little. "We made pictures."

"Did the teacher ask you to draw pictures?"

I shook my head. "It was spelling."

"So you were drawing pictures instead of writing spelling words?" Mr. Conwell said.

"Yes."

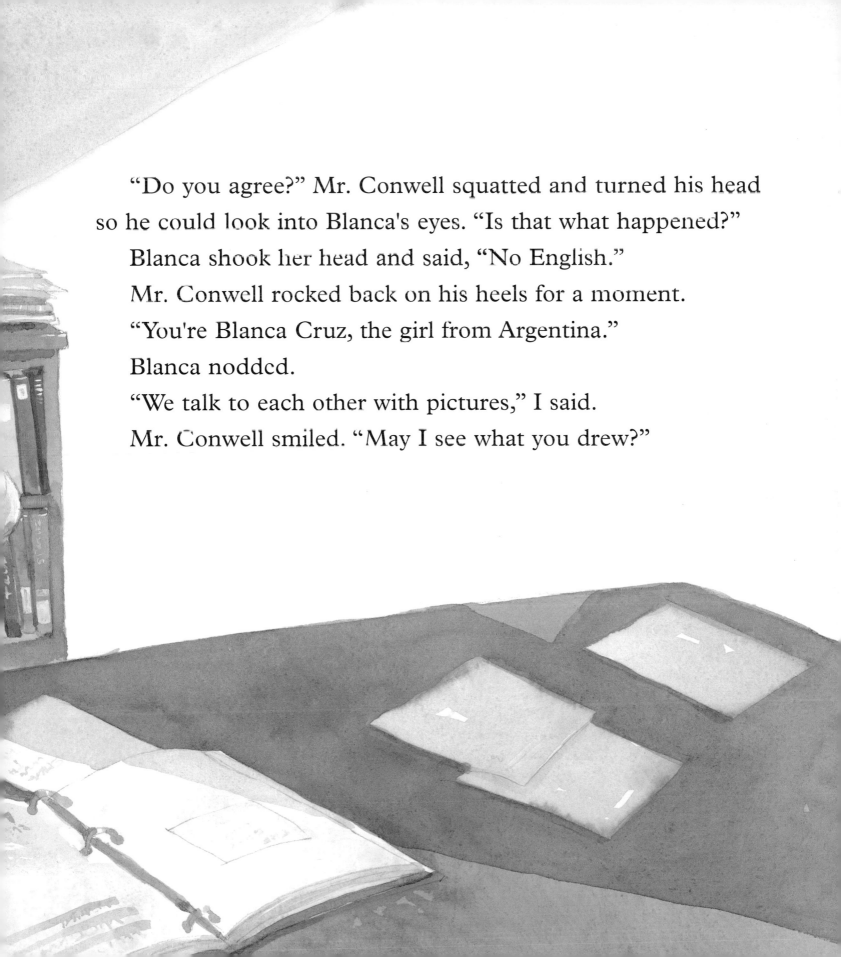

"Do you agree?" Mr. Conwell squatted and turned his head so he could look into Blanca's eyes. "Is that what happened?"

Blanca shook her head and said, "No English."

Mr. Conwell rocked back on his heels for a moment.

"You're Blanca Cruz, the girl from Argentina."

Blanca nodded.

"We talk to each other with pictures," I said.

Mr. Conwell smiled. "May I see what you drew?"

The next day our pictures were hanging on the wall outside the office door. We heard nice things from students and teachers. Mrs. Bertram gave us a compliment and a warning.

"Remember what you promised Mr. Conwell. No more drawing during class time."

Lots of days have passed since then. Blanca sits with me and the other second grade girls at lunch. She plays outside with us at recess. Blanca has taught us Spanish jump rope rhymes. She doesn't shake her head and say, "No English," anymore. But she does still count in Spanish, "uno, dos, tres. . . ."

We count along with her.